EARLY REA...

Beast Quest

Ravira
Ruler of the Underworld

Ravira, Ruler of the Underworld was
originally published as a Beast Quest special.
This version has been specially adapted for
developing readers in conjunction with a
Reading Consultant.

*You will earn one special gold coin for every chapter
you finish. Find out what to do with your
coins at the back of the book!*

1

With special thanks to Michael Ford and
Fiona Munro

Reading Consultant: Prue Goodwin, lecturer in literacy and
children's books

ORCHARD BOOKS

First published in Great Britain in 2011 by Orchard Books
This edition published in 2016 by The Watts Publishing Group

1 3 5 7 9 10 8 6 4 2

Text © Beast Quest Limited 2011, 2016

Cover and inside illustrations by Lee Carey © Beast Quest Limited 2011, 2016

Beast Quest is a registered trademark of Beast Quest Limited
Series created by Beast Quest Limited, London

The moral rights of the author and illustrator have been asserted.

A CIP catalogue record for this book is available from the British Library.

ISBN 978 1 40834 184 1

Printed in China

The paper and board used in this book are made from wood
from responsible sources.

Orchard Books
An imprint of Hachette Children's Group
Part of The Watts Publishing Group Limited
Carmelite House, 50 Victoria Embankment, London EC4Y 0DZ

An Hachette UK Company
www.hachette.co.uk

www.hachettechildrens.co.uk

www.beastquest.co.uk

Ravira
Ruler of the Underworld

BY ADAM BLADE

ORCHARD

THE ICY PLAINS

THE NORTHERN
MOUNTAINS

THE CENTRAL
PLAINS

THE FOREST
OF FEAR

GRASSY
PLAINS

WESTERN OCEAN

THE WINDING RIVER

THE RUBY DESERT

SPINDREL

Beasts *of* Avantia

THE PIT OF FIRE

MALVEL'S MAZE

STONEWIN VOLCANO

ERRINEL

THE DEAD VALLEY

THE DEAD JUNGLE

THE DARK WOOD

THE DARK JUNGLE

TOM

Heroic fighter of
Beasts and saviour
of Avantia

ELENNA

Tom's loyal and
trusted friend and
companion

ADURO

The Good Wizard
who serves King
Hugo and guides
Tom

STORM

Tom's brave
stallion

TALADON

Tom's father and
Master of the Good
Beasts of Avantia

SILVER

Elenna's pet wolf
and friend

KING HUGO

King of
Avantia

BO

An Avantian
farmer

JACOB

The brave son
of Bo

RAVIRA

A cruel
underworld
Beast

HOUNDS
OF AVANTIA

Ravira's evil
servants

FERNO

The Fire Dragon.
One of the six Good
Beasts of Avantia

CONTENTS

STORY ONE: THE HOUNDS OF AVANTIA

1. Terrible News   12
2. Taladon   20
3. The Boatman   26
4. Ravira   34

STORY TWO: WELCOME TO THE UNDERWORLD

1. A Hound Bite   44
2. Moonlight   52
3. Ferno to the Rescue   60
4. Transformed   66

STORY ONE

The Hounds of Avantia

My nostrils flare as I send out a howl. Fear spreads through the kingdom. The time has come.

Humans, fear us. Heroes, tremble. The Hounds of Avantia have been unleashed!

Chapter 1
Terrible News

Tom was in his chamber at King Hugo's palace one sunny morning, when Aduro burst in.

"Terrible news!" he said, panting. "Your father, Taladon, is in danger! There has been a disturbance in the village of Shrayton," he went on.

"What kind of disturbance?" Tom asked the Good Wizard.

"A terrible evil," muttered Aduro. "A cursed Beast – Ravira."

Tom suddenly felt the chill of fear.

"Ravira is the most cruel Beast ever to stalk this kingdom," said Aduro. "But she is supposed to stay in the underworld. Your father was bitten by one of her servants – a Hound of Avantia."

"Is my father dead?" asked Tom, quietly.

"He lives," replied Aduro. "But in the light of tonight's moon, he will change and become a Hound of Avantia too. He will then be cursed to live for eternity as a vicious dog, serving the Beast, Ravira."

Suddenly, Tom's friend, Elenna, was at the door. She had heard their anxious voices.

"We must go at once," called Tom, darting from the room with Elenna close behind.

They headed to the stables
to saddle up Tom's faithful
stallion, Storm, and were on
their way. Elenna's loyal wolf,
Silver, ran alongside them.

Storm's powerful legs carried them towards Shrayton. After many hours, they burst onto a muddy track marked with other hoofprints.

"This must be the way," said Elenna.

After a while, a shape appeared far in the distance. Tom let Storm slow his pace and saw that it was a boy.

"Are you Tom?" asked the child. "Taladon told me to expect a boy and a girl on a black horse. I'm Jacob."

Tom jumped down from the saddle. They had arrived. "Where is my father?" he asked.

"Follow me," said Jacob, leading the way towards a stable.

"Quick!" Jacob hissed, hurrying them around the side. Towards the village, they watched a crowd gathering. "They patrol the streets looking for people who've been bitten," said Jacob. "They don't know your father is here."

As the boy pushed the stable
door open, Tom saw Taladon
inside. His wrists were in chains.

"Why have you locked
him up?" Tom asked angrily.
But before Jacob could answer,
Tom's father sprang from
the ground, his face twisted
with rage.

As Tom jumped back in
shock, he saw that thick
hair coated the back of
Taladon's neck.

"What's happened to you?"
Tom asked.

Chapter 2

Taladon

"You shouldn't have come," Taladon croaked. "It's too late." His eyes looked like those of a wild animal.

"I did as he asked," Jacob muttered. "He insisted that I lock him up. He'd seen what happened to the others when they were bitten."

Tom and Elenna looked at him in confusion.

"The next night," Jacob
went on, "when the moon
rises, they turn into Hounds."

"We have to fight Ravira,"
Tom said. "Where is her lair?"

Taladon's reply was lost in a gruesome howl as he began to transform before their eyes.

"Come on, Tom!" cried Elenna. "He can't help us now!"

As they left the stable, Jacob locked the door. Glancing towards Silver, he whispered, "I think I know the way to Ravira, but you should leave the wolf here. Your horse, too."

Tom didn't like the idea of leaving his companions, but at least they would be staying with his father.

Jacob picked up Taladon's
sword and passed it to Tom.

"You should take this," Tom
said, handing it to Elenna.

As they made their way
towards the centre of Shrayton,
Tom felt uneasy.

"Taladon is a great fighter."
Tom frowned. "How did one of
these Hounds get close enough
to bite him?"

"He went to help a farmer
who had been bitten," explained
Jacob.

They paused just by a well in
the main square.

"It all started when the
well dried up," said Jacob in
a hushed voice. "And strange
noises started coming from it."

"Maybe Ravira is lurking
down there," suggested Elenna.

Chapter 3

The Boatman

Tom and Elenna peered down into the well.

"It's narrow enough to climb down," said Tom. "We can press our backs across one wall, our feet against the other."

A flicker of fear crossed Elenna's face.

"My father, Bo, was bitten," said Jacob. "He was the farmer your father went to help.

He has a scar on his cheek.
Please look out for him."

Tom assured him they would
do what they could and then
they lowered themselves down.

It was slow going. Tom was
feeling tired when stones began
falling onto them from above.

Elenna lost her balance and fell, smashing into Tom. He lost his grip and they both dropped like stones into the blackness. A moment later, they were sliding down a muddy slope. Shocked and winded, Tom tried to slow himself down as he caught sight of something terrifying ahead.

It was a bubbling pool of
fire. With desperate force, he
managed to sink his sword into
the mud and gradually came to
a halt.

Elenna slammed into him and,
trembling, they got to their feet
and stared at the lake of lava in
front of them.

"This way," said Tom, pointing along a path made from polished white rock. "It must lead to Ravira."

Together, they walked through the swirling, stinking smoke.

In the dim light, Tom made out a boat drifting towards them. It was manned by a figure in dark cloak.

"Only those who have been bitten may cross to the queen's city," the figure snarled.

Tom thought fast. He pushed the tip of his sword into his leg.

"The Hounds have bitten us," said Tom, showing his wound.

The boatman pulled down his hood, revealing a pale scar down one side of his face.

"You're Jacob's father!" Elenna gasped.

The boatman shot out both hands, dragging Tom and Elenna into the boat. Trying not to panic, they felt themselves slowly moving across the boiling lava.

"Duck!" shouted Tom as arcs of flame shot through the air towards them. Howls and distant thunder echoed all around as the boatman eventually rounded a curve. A city of white stone appeared before them.

As the boatman slid into the shallows, Tom and Elenna leapt out.

"Ravira's Hounds will tear you to pieces," warned the boatman, as he pushed back out onto the fiery lake.

"No turning back now," whispered Tom.

Chapter 4

Ravira

"This must be Ravira's lair," said Tom.

There was no sound as he led the way through the empty streets towards a vast fortress up ahead. There was no sign of life anywhere either.

As they moved into the courtyard, it was darker. The air seemed thick with the smell of animals, like stables or kennels.

As they pressed on, weapons ready, a staircase rose ahead of them. At the very top was a huge throne. On it sat a statue.

"Ravira?" asked Tom.

"Welcome to the underworld," whispered a woman's voice.

As Ravira stood, Tom saw that she was at least seven feet tall. Her skin was tinged with green and her eyes blazed yellow like flaming torches. Around the base of the steps, five Hounds of Avantia stood guard. They looked strong, with thick dark fur. Their teeth were as sharp as daggers. Tom held his shield up. Could they take on five of these creatures without killing them? They were, after all, citizens of Avantia, who had been entranced by Ravira.

Ravira suddenly tipped her
head back into a beam of light.
She was drawing power from
the moonlight!

"We can't risk fighting the Hounds," Elenna said to Tom. "One bite, and we'll go the same way as your father."

"After them!" Ravira suddenly screamed, releasing the dogs from their leashes.

Tom grabbed Elenna's hand and they raced back out into the strange white city. The pack of snapping Hounds was right behind them.

Elenna pointed to a tall turret. "If we climb up, they won't be able to follow," she said, panting.

They threw themselves
against the wall, the Hounds
on their heels. Feeling around
for handholds, Tom and Elenna
scrambled up the rough stone.

It wasn't long before Tom
heard a terrible crumbling sound.

Welcome to the Underworld

I feel the power of the moon over me. I feel Ravira's spirit take me over completely. I am a man no more. Soon Ravira will reign over all.

Ravira's faithful servant,
Taladon

Chapter 1
A Hound Bite

Tom hit the ground hard. Dust filled his eyes and throat and rocks smashed into his limbs. He thought he could hear Elenna screaming. Then all was quiet.

"Elenna!" he called.

Tom tried to move his arms and legs. But he was trapped.

A shaft of light appeared through the fallen stones. Tom heard sounds coming from above.

Then Tom smelled the animal scent of the Hounds.

"No!" he suddenly heard Elenna whimper from nearby.

He reached for the hilt of his sword just as he felt a huge slab lifted away above his head.

Peering round towards the
light, Tom came face to face
with one of Ravira's Hounds.
Drool dripped onto Tom's

cheek as the Hound snapped its teeth into his arm. He cried out as the sharp fangs sank through his skin.

"I've been bitten!" he called out, glancing down at the deep gashes on his arm.

Almost at once, a strange feeling spread down his arm, across his chest and through his body, right to the tips of his toes. The dog's eyes were filled with evil.

More Hounds appeared above Tom, pawing away the stones.

One of the drooling monsters leaned down and gripped the collar of Tom's tunic, dragging him from the rubble.

"Tom?" said Elenna.

Tom saw his friend being held by another of the Hounds. Her clothes were torn and her face was covered in dust. Glancing down, he noticed the same teeth marks through her trousers.

"I feel different," she said.

A sense of dread filled Tom.

He wondered how long they had to save themselves, to save everyone, to defeat Ravira.

The Hounds dragged Tom and Elenna away from the tower and back towards the fortress. . .and their mistress.

A single column of moonlight shone down onto Ravira's throne. She pointed a bony finger at Tom and Elenna. "Welcome back, my children!" she cackled.

Tom saw she held several leashes. A row of Hounds stood waiting by her throne.

"There are more than before," whispered Elenna.

"That's because more people are being bitten all the time," Tom replied.

"Meet your brothers and sisters," said Ravira.

Tom drew his sword and glared at the Evil Beast.

"While there's blood in my veins, I'll never be one of them," he shouted.

Chapter 2
Moonlight

Suddenly, a bright beam of moonlight fell directly onto Tom and Elenna. Screaming, they shielded their eyes and dropped to their knees. They writhed in pain as the light burned their skin.

"What is this?" cried Tom.

"That was just a little taste of what is to come," said Ravira.

The Hounds snarled and strained on their leashes.

Tom felt completely desperate.
There had to be a way to reach
Ravira. If she was under some
kind of enchantment, perhaps he
could reason with her. "Why are
you doing this?" he asked.

"Silence!" she hissed furiously.

As Ravira moved, just for a moment, out of the moonlight, Tom thought he caught sight of a younger woman – not like a Beast at all. As she moved back into the light, her skin wrinkled again before his eyes.

"You know nothing of my curse!" she whispered.

"The moonlight is the source of all her power!" whispered Elenna.

Ravira laughed as a doorway beside her throne slid open.

A Hound, bigger and more evil-looking than the others, entered the chamber. The look in his eyes chilled Tom's blood.

"Tom," hissed Ravira. "Meet your father."

The Hound snarled and stared at Tom. He was chained but was straining to get free.

"Father?" Tom said.

Tom lifted his shield and the Hound's teeth raked across it.

"Release him from his chains!" Tom shouted at Ravira.

As beams of moonlight shone down through the roof, Tom felt burning across his skin. He could see Elenna falling to her knees in pain too. As the feeling increased, anger rose up in Tom.

Hatred boiled in his heart.

I'm changing, he realised. *And there's nothing I can do.*

"Do you feel it yet?" Ravira smiled. "The thirst for blood?"

As Ravira shouted, Tom noticed something terrible.

"Elenna! Your mouth!"

His friend turned to him. Her teeth were growing longer and sharper. Her face was changing too, in front of his eyes!

"It's time to join the pack!" Ravira laughed.

Pain stabbed across Tom's chest as he saw his father stalking towards him. There had to be some way to stop this. He had to block out the moonlight.

As his father, the Hound, pounced, his face was full of hatred. Reaching out for his sword, Tom felt a sudden urge to hurt him.

"Remember he's your father!" cried Elenna, just in time.

Chapter 3

Ferno to the Rescue

Suddenly, Tom opened his eyes and saw the shape of a huge wing hovering high above.

"Ferno!" called Tom. The great friendly Beast had come to their rescue. He must have sensed their fear. The bulk of the huge dragon kept out the moonlight almost completely.

"What's happening?" Ravira cried. "Hounds! Attack!"

Tom and Elenna tried to fight off the Hounds but time was running out. Soon they would be changed forever.

"Your Quest is over!" cackled Ravira above the growling of her Hounds. She was standing in the last beam of moonlight. "You won't defeat me!"

The Hounds whined in fear as the great Beast flapped his wings overhead and the chamber became dark. One Hound didn't seem as afraid as the others, and took a step towards Tom. Taladon!

"I don't want to fight you," said Tom. But he was ready when the animal jumped towards him.

Tom had no choice, and thrust his sword into his father's side. The creature fell suddenly to the ground.

"What have I done?" Tom
said quietly.

"Call off your dragon,
and I'll spare your lives!" spat
Ravira.

"Never!" replied Tom.

Using his shield, Tom forged a path through the mass of Hounds. He had just reached Ravira's throne when he was thrown to the ground. He twisted round to see a Hound with its sharp teeth gripping his trouser leg. It dragged him across the ground while he kicked it with his other foot. At last it let go.

"There are too many of them!" shouted Elenna. She was slashing at the Beasts to keep them at bay.

"I think Ravira's power is linked to the Hounds as well as the moonlight," Tom replied. "They make her stronger!"

Chapter 4
Transformed

"If I can help you past the Hounds," said Tom to Elenna, "you cut through the leashes."

He scraped the tip of his sword across the stone floor, sending up a shower of sparks. The Hounds retreated in fear.

"Now!" Tom shouted.

Elenna took a few steps then bounded over the Hounds and up the steps towards Ravira.

"Stop her!" yelled the Beast as
Elenna swung Taladon's sword
and brought it down onto the
chains. The leashes burst apart.

The Hounds stopped snarling.
Their red eyes faded to soft grey.

"They are no longer under
her control," Elenna said.

Ravira roared in fury.

"I will come back for you," Tom called to his father as they backed out of the chamber.

The Beast struck at them with the spiked leashes. Tom and Elenna managed to catch the chains around their swords, dragging Ravira with them. Soon they were outside again and nearing the lava lake.

"I'll tear you to pieces!" Ravira shouted. She had turned now, and was trying to pull Tom and Elenna towards her.

They pulled back hard, and
then let the chains go slack.

    With a panicked cry, Ravira
lost her balance and fell,
screaming, into the boiling lake.

Tom turned back at once. He had to save his father.

When they arrived at the fortress, the Hounds blocked their path. Tom took a big risk.

"You're not evil, are you?" he whispered.

The creatures dropped to the ground, seeming to shrink. Their limbs changed shape and their faces turned human again. Soon the chamber was filled with confused people. One of them was Taladon.

"How can we get out?"

asked Elenna. No one wanted
to cross the lava lake. Who knew
what power Ravira still held?

"Follow us," said a voice.
It was Bo, leading the saved
people. "There is another way."

The weary group followed Bo along a low, dark passage until at last they saw light ahead. He pushed open a trap door and they were back in the village of Shrayton.

Riding towards them on Storm was Jacob.

"Your horse wouldn't stop whinnying!" he said. "He seemed to know you'd be here!"

"My son!" said Bo as they were happily reunited at last.

"Avantia's underworld is the darkest place," said a voice.

Aduro was walking towards
them. "But I know that with
heroes such as you fighting for
it, Avantia is well protected."

"Farewell, friends," called
Tom. "Now we must go home."

THE END

If you enjoyed this story, you may want to read

Mortaxe
The Skeleton Warrior

Here's how the story begins...

Tom sighed as he pulled on his robe and looked down at his feet in their sparkling slippers. He didn't feel very comfortable, but it was King Hugo's birthday, and he was a guest at the castle. The clothes had been left in his bedchamber, and a servant had asked him to try the outfit on.

Suddenly, Tom's door flew open. It was Elenna.

"Just look what they've done to me!" she said angrily.

His good friend wore a shimmering yellow dress and had a tiara plonked on the top of her short, spiky hair. Tom tried hard not to giggle.

Suddenly, there was a loud

bang outside and Tom rushed to the window. As Tom looked around, there came another loud noise, but this time an orange light burst above the turrets like a firework.

"Look!" said Elenna, pointing.

Aduro was standing on a patch of bare ground.

"He must be preparing fireworks for the celebrations!" Tom laughed.

Whistling loudly, Tom managed to get the Good

Wizard's attention, just as yet another explosion rattled the windows and shook the walls.

Tom frowned. This was not a firework display. This was something else. Something bad.

As smoke rose into the sky, Aduro began to run.

READ

Mortaxe

The Skeleton Warrior

EARLY READER

TO FIND OUT WHAT HAPPENS NEXT!

LEARN TO READ WITH

EARLY READER

Beast Quest

Beast Quest Early Readers are easy-to-read versions of the bestselling Beast Quest books, specially adapted for developing readers

Perfect for parents to read aloud and for newly confident readers to read along

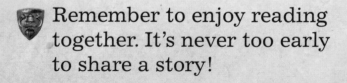
Remember to enjoy reading together. It's never too early to share a story!

Series 1
COLLECT THEM ALL!

Meet Tom, Elenna and the first six Beasts!

FERNO
THE FIRE DRAGON

978-1-84616-483-5

SEPRON
THE SEA SERPENT

978-1-84616-482-8

ARCTA
THE MOUNTAIN GIANT

978-1-84616-484-2

TAGUS
THE HORSE-MAN

978-1-84616-486-6

NANOOK
THE SNOW MONSTER

978-1-84616-485-9

EPOS
THE FLAME BIRD

978-1-84616-487-3

CONGRATULATIONS, YOU HAVE COMPLETED THIS QUEST!

At the end of each chapter you were awarded a special gold coin. The QUEST in this book was worth an amazing **8** coins.

Look at the Beast Quest totem picture inside the back cover of this book to see how far you've come in your journey to become

MASTER OF THE BEASTS.

The more books you read, the more coins you will collect!

Do you want your own Beast Quest Totem?

1. Copy the coin below
2. Go to the Beast Quest website
3. Download and print out your totem
4. Add your coin to the totem

www.beastquest.co.uk/totem

31901060002211